THE NIGHT ONES

by Patricia Grossman   illustrated by Lydia Dabcovich

HARCOURT BRACE JOVANOVICH, PUBLISHERS

San Diego   New York   London

Library of Congress Cataloging-in-Publication Data
Grossman, Patricia.
The night ones/by Patricia Grossman;
illustrated by Lydia Dabcovich. — 1st ed.
p.   cm.
Summary: The night bus carries people who
work at night to their jobs — in an office
building, a bakery, a hotel, an airport,
and a dockyard — and the morning
bus takes them home again.
ISBN 0-15-257438-7
[1. Night work — Fiction.   2. Occupations — Fiction.]
I. Dabcovich, Lydia, ill.   II. Title.
PZ7.G9087Ni   1991
[E] — dc20   89-19815

First edition
A B C D E

The illustrations in this book were done in
markers and Prismacolor pencils on tissue paper.

The display type was set in Gill Sans Medium.

The text type was set in Gill Sans Medium.

Composition by Thompson Type, San Diego, California

Color separations were made by Bright Arts, Ltd., Singapore.

Printed and bound by Tien Wah Press, Singapore

Production supervision by Warren Wallerstein and Ginger Boyer

Designed by Judythe Sieck

For my niece, Rachel —P. G.   *For Mu* —L. D.

When the night bus arrives at the stop the night ones get off

and turn down the street.

They walk until Clarence says good night

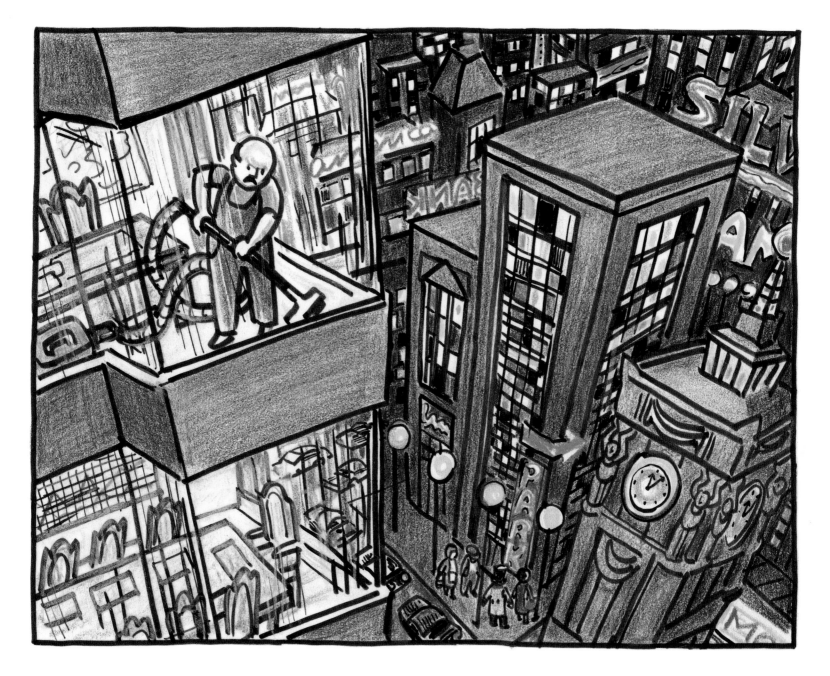

and goes off to clean important rooms.

Four move along until it is time for Honey to leave

and begin rolling her night away.

Three continue until Porter says farewell

and goes to greet travelers from near and far.

Two walk steadily along

until Amelia catches another bus,

which takes her to her office,

the sky.

Only Cap is left and he runs to the docks,

where a ship heads in, sailing west.

The night ones stay in their places . . .

. . .

. . .

. . .

. . . until morning.

Then Cap watches a ship head out,
sailing east;

Amelia turns her back on the office that circles the world;

Porter tips his hat to Oscar, who will hold the door all day;

Honey greets the avenue with a heavenly smell;

and Clarence spins himself out the last important door.

When the night ones reach their stop

the night bus pulls away to make room for the morning bus,

which takes them home.